MOUNT-*Me*

ANNELISE REYNOLDS

Copyright

© 2021 Annelise Reynolds
Mount Me

For questions or comments about this book, please contact the author at:

authorannelisereynolds@gmail.com
Editor: Ryder Editing and Formatting
Cover Designer: Sweet 15 Designs

Contents

Prologue

Natalia

"Almost done for the day." I smiled at Kelly, the hairstylist who had been changing my hair from one outfit to the next. It had been a long day in front of the camera, and I was ready to get home for the night.

"Yes. Thank God," I said, trying to cover a yawn. We'd been at this since just after sunrise. Next time I was going to tell my agent to limit it to two shoots in a single day. Three was too much, and I felt a migraine starting to form at the back of my neck.

"It's been crazy today, but that guy you did the last spread with. He's new, right? He's totally hot." I've worked with Kelly a few times before on shoots, and she's excellent. One of the more easygoing girls in the business. I've been modeling since I was seventeen, and five years later, I'm starting to get tired and burnout.

"Derik," I offered his name. "Yeah, he's new to the business and good looking." He was also an egomaniac and shallow. I spent the afternoon in various stages of dress and outfits with him.

Sometimes in an outdoor bed on the beach and other times in the sand. No matter what we did or talked about, he always turned the focus back on him. He wouldn't last long if he didn't check his ego. Nobody wanted to work with a know it all, self-absorbed asshat.

If Kelly thought he was sexy and that we had chemistry on camera, then I'd done my job well because I couldn't wait for that segment of the shoots to be done for the day.

My next set was on the beach wearing a teal designer bikini in the middle of winter. It would be cold, but I just wanted to get it over with.

"Hey, Nat," Brenna, my assistant, came into the trailer. "You've got flowers, hon."

She was holding a box of flowers. When I opened them, there were six gorgeous red roses.

"Who are they from?" Kelly asked, spraying hairspray in my hair.

"It doesn't say who it's from. All it says is, *I think you're beautiful.*"

"And there's no name?" Brenna asked, taking the half dozen flowers from me.

"No. There's no name. Maybe the person that sent them is shy?"

"The flowers are gorgeous."

"Yes. I wish I knew who to thank for sending them." I shrugged. "Brenna, can you put them in some water for me? I need to get out there to finish this shoot."

"Sure."

I brushed off the flowers and the note, but I didn't realize it was just the beginning.

Chapter One

Natalia

"I'm getting off the plane now. Is the house set up for me?"

"Yeah, Honey. Are you sure you don't want to stay with us?" My mom was worried about me, and she had every right to be. I had a stalker, somebody lurking in the shadows—watching me. The last six months had been the most nerve racking of my life, ever since I got that first package.

The first letter and rose I didn't take seriously, in fact I thought it was sweet that someone had sent me an anonymous letter telling me how much they loved my photos. That sweetness turned into creepy very quickly. Six months went by, and each month I got a letter with another rose added to it. The letters were getting more possessive, and I was starting to get scared.

After being away from home for five years, I was back. The bitter cold of Canada was a shock to my California acclimated system. I'd left home at seventeen when I sent my pictures into a modeling agency and someone had contacted me wanting to represent me. In five years, I'd gone from a no name Canadian kid to an international supermodel recognized around the globe. It was my dream to get out of my little town in Alberta to see the world, and I did.

Mom and dad flew down to LA a few times to see me, but this was the first time I was coming home. I didn't realize how much I missed it until I got off the plane and saw the beautiful snow-covered landscape of Edmonton.

"I'm sure, Mom. I don't want you guys to get caught up in all of this."

"You're my daughter, Nat. It's my job to protect you."

"I know, Mom, but I couldn't live with myself if something happened to you."

We'd talked about this a few times over the last few weeks while I ran across the US on different flights, trying to hide myself from this guy. My long, curly, blonde locks that I was known for were gone. I had a short, sassy, chocolate cherry-colored bob now. Paranoia was setting in because I was almost to the point of walking away from modeling if this guy wasn't caught.

"Natalia, I need to tell you something."

"Yes?" I questioned hesitantly.

"Are you at the baggage claim yet?"

I smiled, thinking that they were here to pick me up. It was just like them to do that. God, I missed my parents so much. I stayed away far too long.

"Are you here?" I guessed picking up the pace to get there. all of a sudden homesickness swamped me and I wanted to hug my parents so hard that the broken pieces of myself would fit back together.

"No, we aren't. We are waiting for you at the rental, but we sent a friend to get you."

"A friend?" I asked skeptically. "Uncle E?" I guessed. Elijah Edwards wasn't technically my uncle. He was my dad's best friend from back in the day. They were as close as brothers, and I grew up calling him Uncle E because when I was a young girl, I couldn't say Elijah, so it stuck.

"No. It's not Uncle E. It's Uncle E's son of sorts."

Uncle Elijah and his wife Madison didn't have kids. They weren't able to have them, even though they tried for years. Eventually they adopted a girl, Avery, but she was probably only about ten years old now.

"Who?" I stepped on the escalator, my purse hung across my body, and the hood of my jacket pulled up to help hide my identity. I wanted to make sure that nobody saw me or made a fuss about me being back in Canada. The last thing that I needed was the tabloids spouting my location to the world.

"His name is Gavin. He's a Mountie. I'll explain the rest when you get home."

"Mom, what did you do?"

Her voice broke as she said, "We just want you safe, Nat." I could hear the tears in her voice as she choked back sobs. "I just want my baby safe."

Mom hung up the phone, and I started to worry about what I was about to get myself into. What plans had she made with this Gavin guy? Who was he to Uncle E? Why had I never heard of him before? But most importantly, what the hell was my mother up to?

Chapter Two

Gavin

I couldn't believe that Elijah talked me into this. Natalia Van Buren was every man's fantasy. The supermodel was sure to draw attention wherever she went, and that attention would also put me in the spotlight. A place that was just as dangerous for me as it was for her right now.

Fuck. Who knew that Elijah's niece was the world's hottest supermodel? I owed the man my life, so I'd do anything he asked of me, but damn, babysitting while recouping from a gunshot wound wasn't high on my list of things.

I figured my few months off would be spent watching sports and drinking beer, not watching over the woman I'd been secretly picturing in my dreams and jacking off to for the last couple years. My dick was already twitching just thinking about being near her in person for any amount of time.

Elijah told me to meet her by the baggage claim and to observe before I approached her, because I needed to make sure she wasn't followed from the last leg of her journey. When she came down the escalator, I almost didn't recognize her.

"*Good girl*," I acknowledged silently. She'd changed her look and camouflaged herself the best she could. If it weren't for those turquoise eyes, I'd never have recognized her. Her eyes were a dead giveaway of her identity.

I watched her as she hung up the phone and went to the baggage claim to get her bags. She was in jeans, boots, and a hoodie. A thick winter coat was over her arm, and her purse was hooked across her body. She was dressed to blend in, and nobody seemed to be looking at her except for me.

After giving the room a final scan and watching her take her bags as they passed, I approached her. Hey, Nat, I'm Gavin. Did you talk to your mom t?"

She jumped, then looked over at me, her eyes ning slightly from the startle I gave her. "Yes."

Good. How many bags do you have? We need ɒ moving," I said, looking away from her and g the surrounding crowd again.

t these three bags." She motioned to the er feet. One big suitcase with two smaller er carry-on.

ll get the big one and the carry on. Can those two or do we need to get a cart?" nage."

"Good, come on. We are too exposed here." I grabbed the carry on and hooked it over my good shoulder and took the bigger suitcase from her.

I stayed by her side and led her toward the nearest exit. The smell of strawberries tickled my nose as I leaned toward her to cut through the crowd. Being here was dangerous, not only for her, but for me. People were looking for me, dangerous people that would like nothing more than to have me buried six feet under.

"How did you get roped into picking me up?" she asked when we stopped near the door long enough for her to put on her heavier jacket.

"I owe Elijah one, and I'm off on medical leave."

Her eyes looked over me like she didn't think I was hurt, and I wanted to keep it that way. My arm was screaming at me since I took it out of the sling, and I was being careful not to use it too much, but I wanted to appear like I was one hundred percent healed and capable to anyone that may be watching.

"I'm ready," she said, picking the two bags back up. When we went outside, she sucked in a sharp breath as the frigid air swirled around us. Snow covered the ground. But we would be getting more in the days to come.

"Crap." She gasped and pulled her arms tighter to her body. "I forgot how this feels."

"LA will do that to you." I led her to the tram that would take us right up to my truck. The faster we got on the road, the better and safer I'd feel.

We got to the truck quickly. I used my key fob to start it before we got close and to get the heater going. I didn't see anyone paying attention to us, and as soon as we got to the truck and her stuff loaded, I started to relax a bit.

"So, what all did your mom tell you?" I asked as I backed out of the parking spot.

"Nothing. She said she was waiting for me at the rental, and that you would be taking me there."

"Okay," I confirmed, but it wasn't the full truth. Yes, we were going to the rental, and yes, her parents were there, but she made it sound like I was leaving her there and that's where she was wrong.

The rental was a small two-story house in a quiet neighborhood in Fort McMurray. We had a two-hour drive ahead of us, and I didn't want to be sitting next to a pissed off woman for those two hours, so I didn't fill her in on the rest of the plan.

Chapter Three

Natalia

What was going on? I was still suspicious of the turn of events, but mom had said Gavin was taking me home, so I trusted him because she, dad, and uncle E did. I just wondered why I'd never seen or heard about the sexy Mountie before, and Gavin was definitely sexy.

He had a long, lean runner's build, and his tall frame was big enough to make me feel small and dainty next to him, which was no easy feat since I was five foot eleven. Gavin's hair was a medium brown, and his eyes were golden brown. He had a classic good-looking square jaw, and his nose was slightly bent from being broken before. In a word, he was hot. Hot in a way that just came naturally to him.

"How were you injured?" I finally broke the silence to ask a question. We had two hours ahead of us, and I was curious about the guy next to me.

"Gunshot wound to the chest. It's why I couldn't carry all your bags."

"Oh, that's okay. Thank you for taking the ones you did. Chivalry isn't dead, I guess." I shrugged and looked out the window. We were leaving the city and headed north. The streets were plowed, but the snow was picking up.

"Maybe I should have flown directly into Fort McMurray," I said when he made the wipers go faster. He was driving slowly, not pushing the truck too fast for the weather.

"You did good making your journey last over the week, Natalia. If this guy is following you, that made it more difficult for him. Changing your hair and appearance helped, too. You were smart to do it the way you did. The weather is just a small bump in the road."

"Do you think we will make it back to Fort McMurray tonight?" I wanted to be home where it was warm and safe. God, I wanted to be safe. The last time I felt truly ok was months ago. Since then, sleeping and eating have been almost nonexistent. That's why I decided to take a break from that world.

"We should if it doesn't get any worse than this. Did you happen to bring copies of the letters your stalker sent?"

"No. I don't ever want to see those notes again." I shuddered over the memory and put my hands closer to the vents to seek their warmth.

"I'll see if I can get in touch with the investigators on the case down there. Not sure they will cooperate or give me anything, but if I can at least get a copy of the letters, I can try to pull some information about our stalker from them."

"You think you will be able to figure out something they didn't?" I asked skeptically. The police had the letters for three months. The third one was where I realized he was getting creepier with each gift. It was the sixth letter that had my blood running cold.

"It never hurts to have more eyes on it." He shrugged. "The sooner we can catch your stalker, the sooner your life returns to normal."

Normal. My life wasn't normal anymore, it was a giant mess. The problem with getting everything you ever wanted sometimes is that you aren't prepared for the new normal that life creates.

"How long are you on medical leave?" I asked, changing the subject back to him.

He didn't answer at first, and I wondered if he was going to ignore the question, but he didn't. "I'll be on leave for a while. The bullet did some major damage to my shoulder."

"Oh, that sucks."

"Yeah, but it is what it is."

"So, you're in the Mounties with Uncle E. Is that how you know him?"

"No. I'm a Mountie because of him. Elijah saved my life." He didn't expand on that or offer up any more details, and I didn't push for any.

"What's your last name?"

"Kinkaid."

This had to be the most awkward trip ever. I made a mental note to give my mom a hard time when I saw her. Gavin's short and simple answers were driving me nuts. He didn't ask questions about me unless it pertained to the stalker. When I asked questions to try to initiate conversation, he answered the questions but didn't reciprocate. It was like playing table tennis by yourself—useless and not as much fun.

"You do realize I'm trying to make conversation with you, right?" It was a little bitchy, but seriously, I was on a whole new level of tired and hungry.

He glanced in my direction with a small smirk. "I'm aware, Natalia, but I'm trying to concentrate on the road and make sure nobody's tailing us. I'm sorry if that bores you, but I'd rather us arrive in one piece.

Well shit, he was right. He didn't deserve my attitude. I shouldn't take my frustration out on him, but for some reason, he made me want to.

I felt on edge and cranky around him, and I'm not sure why. "Sorry," I mumbled, leaning my head against the window. "I'm going to take a nap so you can concentrate."

"Sure thing, Princess."

I leaned the seat back and curled up as much as the seat and belt would allow. It wasn't the most comfortable, but it damn sure beat the seats on the airplane.

"Thanks for picking me up, Kinkaid," I said around a yawn, but I didn't hear his answer because I was already being pulled down into an exhausted, peace-filled, dreamless sleep—something I hadn't had in months.

Chapter Four

Gavin

"Natalia?" I shook her shoulder softly, trying to wake her up. If I was fully healed, I would have attempted to carry her inside, but there was no way I was going to be able to do that, and we needed to get inside because the snowstorm was coming in faster and heavier than they anticipated. "Wake up, Princess. Time to go inside."

I unbuckled her seatbelt and leaned in, brushing the shorter, darker strands of her hair away from her face. Natalia Van Buren was a stunning woman. Her delicate features were soft, her lips were plush and made for kissing, and her body was slightly curved in all the right places. She was what society called a plus-size model, but she just looked perfect to me.

My dick agreed, but I had to ignore the bastard because she was a case, like any other. Plus, getting involved with her would compromise my safety. I shook her again and her brows furrowed. The temperature was dropping outside, and we needed to get in for the night.

"Natalia," I said again, louder and with more firmness in my voice.

She grumbled at me and I laughed. The woman didn't wake up easily, so there was only one thing left to do.

I turned the truck off and opened the door.

Natalia popped up quickly when the cold air stole any warmth that was in the cabin of the truck.

"That was mean," she muttered and opened the truck door, hopping down from the cab.

"I tried to wake you nicely first." I shrugged, trying to hide my laughter at her expense.

"God, it's so cold." She rubbed her fingers together and opened the back door to get her bags. Her parent's car that had been in the garage earlier was gone, so I assumed they left before the snow got too bad.

"Come on." I led her in the house through the garage door. The alarm beeped, and I went to the pad to disable and reset it.

"Mom? Dad?" she called out as soon as she walked in the door.

"They must have left before the storm got too bad," I said, shrugging out of my jackets.

"Let me call them." She reached for her phone and dialed her parents.

Her dad's voice came on the phone. "Hey, Nat. Did you make it to the house?"

"Yeah, where are you guys?"

"I'm sorry, Sweetie. We had to leave because the storm was picking up."

"You guys could've stayed here with me, so I don't have to be alone."

"Alone? Isn't Gavin there with you?"

I stood in the kitchen with my back to the counter, waiting for her to figure out that I wasn't going anywhere.

She was in my temporary home. We were both going to lie low together, but she hadn't figured it out yet and her parents were beating around the bush on telling her. I expect that was because she was stubborn. They wanted to make sure there was no way she could hop on another plane.

I saw the fire in her eyes and the stubborn set in her chin when she thought I was ignoring her to be rude and standoffish. She didn't realize how bad it was snowing and that we honestly should have stayed in Edmonton until the storm passed, but I'd gone ahead and ignored my better judgment and got us home as quickly as possible. She slept through the bad parts of the trip, and I was grateful for that because there at the end it was bad.

"Yes, but he's leaving as soon as the storm lets up, and I wanted to see you guys." Her voice choked up on unshed tears, and I felt bad for her.

"Honey, Gavin's not leaving you. He's staying there to protect you."

"What?" She looked over at me in shock, and I just shrugged. "He's a stranger. You want me to live with a stranger while I'm hiding from a stalker?"

"Well, he's safe and you need someone to help. Since you won't stay with us, we made other arrangements. The storm coming in only helped our cause because now, there's no way you can be stubborn and leave."

Natalia bit her bottom lip and the look on her face said that was exactly what she would have done had the storm not been so bad.

"We'll come see you when the storm has passed, and it's safe to drive. Until then, you are safe. That's what is most important."

They said their goodbyes and hung up the phone. She didn't wait to turn on me. The spark of fire I'd seen in her eyes was burning brighter now.

"You could have warned me."

"I could have," I agreed, but her parents were right. She was a stubborn brat and would have tried to change the situation if given the opportunity. I didn't feel like giving her that chance.

"Why didn't you?"

I pushed away from the counter and moved toward her. When I was close, I caught that whiff of strawberries again. "Because I didn't want to drive for two hours with a pissed off woman in my front seat. It was better to wait until we were here, and your parents could deal with it."

Her pulse fluttered in her neck, and she licked her lips. She didn't have the same kind of fear in her eyes that I'd seen when I first saw her at the airport. This fear was one of curiosity and arousal, and I leaned toward her to reach behind her, but I could hear her suck in a breath at my nearness.

When my hand closed around the bottle of water on the shelf behind her, I straightened and walked away.

"I would have moved out of your way," she grumbled.

"Yeah, but this was more fun, Princess," I called out. "I'm going to sweep the house and let Zeke out of his kennel. Once it's all clear, you can have the master bedroom."

I enter her room and bathroom before heading into the hallway bathroom and bedroom. Finally, I went into the spare room that I'd set my stuff in when I first got here. A large kennel took up most of the smaller bedroom. Zeke was laying down, but as soon as I opened the door his head popped up with excitement.

"You ready to go potty, Boy?"

He barked a yes. His hind end was shaking with excitement at seeing me. I opened his kennel and let him out. Tail wagging, he headed out of the bedroom and straight into the kitchen to find out who the new person he was smelling was.

"Oh," I heard her say as I rounded the corner to find Zeke wrapped up in a hug from Natalia. *Lucky dog*, I thought to myself. "Who are you handsome?" She smiled, running her hand over Zeke's thick fur coat.

"Zeke," I answered her question. He was eating up the attention and seemed to really like her. Most of the time, he wasn't as welcoming with strangers, but for whatever reason, he was enjoying the attention from Natalia.

"The house is clear. I'm going to let the dog out. You can get settled in the master bedroom."

"Okay. Thanks, Gavin."

Chapter Five

Natalia

I liked his dog, but there was something about Gavin Kinkaid that was driving me crazy. I couldn't put a finger on what these feelings were that he was evoking in me because it was unlike anything I'd ever felt before.

When he'd gotten close to me, my skin prickled with awareness. It was weird because I've literally been almost naked with male models before and they never elicited that kind of response from me. They never made my body tense with nerves, and I was supposed to know how to act around Gavin.

It was laughable. I had no clue how to act around him. My experience with men was limited to a few dates and social events. Even in the modeling world, a lot of the men I came in contact with didn't care about me because they were checking each other out. I mean, I had some great friends in those guys, but no prospects for anything more.

I'd been on a few dates with people outside the fashion industry. Grayson Masters was a movie star, and we went out a few times, but I didn't feel any excitement with him. In fact, being on his arm just put me even more in the spotlight which I didn't want. I dated a drummer, but that crashed and burned quickly because he wanted to move faster than I did.

So, I was a twenty-two-year-old virgin supermodel. Handling men and knowing what they were all about was not my forte. Most of my dates to functions were set up for PR purposes. The guys didn't pique my interest or curiosity, not like Gavin did.

I looked at the clock on my phone; it was seven and my stomach was growling. I wondered if Gavin was hungry, too. Do I shower and get into pajamas first, or do I just go make something to eat?

A shower sounded lovely, and after traveling all day, I decided that came first because after I got food in my stomach; I was probably going to crash hard. I was still tired as hell and felt like I could probably sleep for days.

Making my decision, I lifted my big suitcase onto the bed and pulled out my pajamas and toiletry bag. I'd start putting stuff away where it belonged later. Right now, my priorities were shower, food, and sleep.

I grabbed my things and headed into the bathroom. It was a nice size master bath, and I made a note to try out the big jacuzzi garden tub later. Exhaustion was catching up to me fast, and I felt myself fading, so I kept my shower short, going through my routine as quickly as possible.

When I stepped out, I wrapped a fluffy towel around my body and used the other one to dry my hair. The shorter, edgier look was cute. I liked it, but it wasn't what I was used to. It would take a while for me to get used to the new style and color.

I ran a brush through my hair and dried off before grabbing my winter pajamas. I'd packed my footie giraffe pajamas, thinking I'd be either staying with only my parents or by myself. I didn't anticipate Gavin, and my nightgown from Little Big Girls was not something I wanted to wear with him in the house, plus it was too damn cold for my favorite nightie, so being a giraffe was my best option.

Once I was dressed in my jammies, I looked in the mirror and second guessed myself. Should I change into something else until I came back in here? I decided I should, so I stripped out of my pajamas and put on a pair of jeans and a thick sweater so I could skip my bra. Pajamas were for the bedroom only. I didn't want Gavin making fun of me and giving me a hard time about my pajamas like some of my friends did.

Once I was dressed, I went back into the kitchen. Gavin was already in there with Zeke by his side.

The husky had beautiful coloring and his eyes were that beautiful icy blue that huskies were known for.

"I hope you aren't a vegetarian or anything. I didn't grocery shop for any special diets."

I rolled my eyes. "I'm a plus size model for a reason. I like food."

He grinned. "That's good. I'm not going overboard tonight because it's so late, so I hope grilled cheese sandwiches are good with you? If not, we have cereal."

"Grilled cheese is perfect. Thank you."

I watched as he worked on our sandwiches. He cooked them over the gas range and made them the perfect golden-brown color on the outside. We had chips and a bottle of water on the side, and I grabbed a few pickle spears from the fridge because pickles and grilled cheese go together like peanut butter and jelly.

We ate in companionable silence, but I was fading fast. After the third yawn, I decided it was time for me to go to bed before I fell face first into the last bit of my food.

"That was good. Thank you." I moved to the trashcan and dumped the remnants of the food in. I was going to wash the plate, but Gavin stopped me.

"Go to bed, Natalia. You look like you're about to fall over."

"I feel like that."

"Go get some rest. I'll take care of the dishes." I nodded and set the plate in the sink before going back to my room. By the time I had my pajamas back on, I could barely keep my eyes open.

I crawled under the covers and fell asleep thinking about Gavin and the warm fuzzy feeling he made me feel deep in my belly.

Chapter Six

Gavin

After Natalia went to bed, I did the dishes and checked the house again. Everything was locked up tight, so I downed a pain pill and went to bed. Zeke would let me know if there was any threat in the house, so I wasn't worried. If the storm didn't keep her stalker or the Toxic Bastards MC away from us, then Zeke would give me a heads up.

It was a while before the pain pills kicked in enough for me to relax. I spent that time thinking about the woman in the next room. She was everything I didn't need right now.

I knew she was hot and would be tempting, but I didn't know I'd be attracted to other aspects of her personality. She was just the right amount of sweet and sassy, bratty, and a big girl. She called to the Daddy side of me, but I had no idea if she even knew that she was doing it.

My dick had been rock hard since I saw her in the airport. I'd seen men glance at her in appreciation, but she seemed oblivious to it. None of them realized who she was, nor did they pay any special attention to her other than to look her body over.

She said she was a plus size model, and I guess in that industry she would be. Personally, I liked a woman with curves. She had breasts that would bounce as she rode my cock, and hips that I could grip as I pounded her from behind. I ground my teeth together as my cock pulsed with need.

This unofficial assignment was going to keep my cock hard and my balls blue. I already had one cold shower since we got here, and I was now hard again. I took a deep breath, flipping the blankets off me. There was only one way to get comfortable, and I knew that getting off would help me sleep better too.

I spit in my hand and reached into my boxers, freeing my cock from the confines of the material. The warmth of my hand around my shaft had me closing my eyes, imagining it was Natalia's. I pictured her between my legs, sucking on my cock like a popsicle.

The slide of my hand along my length would be nothing compared to her mouth, or better yet, her pussy. I groaned, thinking about pumping into her tight wet sheath. God, she would squeeze my dick so good. I pictured her riding my cock, her breasts bouncing as she rode me hard with her head thrown back as she came all over my cock.

My balls tightened as I kept pumping my length into the tightness of my fist. When I felt the orgasm building at the base of my shaft, I held my other hand over the tip of my cock to catch my cum.

I ground my teeth as my orgasm pulsed, releasing rope after rope of cum into my hand. It was powerful and sent shivers of ecstasy racing down my spine. I'd never come so hard or so long in my life. I kept pumping my cock until it was too sensitive to touch anymore.

It took a minute for my pulse to slow down and the adrenaline spike to ease off. It had been over an hour since she'd gone to bed, so I didn't bother to put clothes on. I went to the hallway bathroom and washed my hands.

When I came out, I saw a faint glow of light coming from the kitchen. Zeke wasn't going crazy or growling, so I knew it was Natalia. Part of me was saying just go to your room and shut the door, but the other part of me, my cock, was saying something else entirely. How the hell my dick was still ready to go when I just rubbed one out, I don't have a fucking clue?

Curiosity and my dick won over. I walked down the hall and flipped the lights in the living room on. Zeke came toward me, his body shaking with excitement at seeing us both up. The poor boy wanted to play, but it was too cold outside right now, and I was too damn tired. I would have to make sure to throw his favorite toy with him tomorrow.

"Zeke, I didn't know you knew any giraffes." I smirked, taking in Natalia's footed pajamas. If I needed any confirmation that she had a Little side, it was gone.

"Shit." Her face flushed red in embarrassment, and I couldn't help but enjoy it. I moved closer to the kitchen, hiding my lower half behind the kitchen island. "I was thirsty, and I thought you'd be asleep," she said, stumbling her way through her explanation.

"I was waiting for my pain pill to kick in," I explained, leaving out the part that I just beat one off and was picturing her while I did it.

"You're hurting?" Her embarrassment disappeared, replaced by concern.

"Yes." *In more ways than one,* I added silently. "I didn't take a pain pill this morning because I knew I'd be driving to Edmonton and back."

"I'm sorry. I didn't know."

"Princess, you didn't know I existed, let alone that I'd be picking you up at the airport today. No need for you to apologize for something you have no control over."

She nodded slightly. "How did you get shot?"

"I was undercover, trying to take down a drug ring. My cover was blown, and they shot me."

Her eyes were wide as her gaze roamed over me. "Where?" she asked quietly. I looked down, my dick was obviously hard, there would be no hiding him if she came around the island to see my wound.

Taking a breath, I lifted my shirt, pulling it over my arms. I gritted my teeth against the pain that shot through my shoulder. I really needed to rest the damn thing.

Natalia's eyes roamed over my chest and landed on the angry scarring by my shoulder. "I was lucky. The bullet went straight through, not hitting any bone, just tearing up all the soft tissue on its way out. Eventually, I'll make a full recovery and be back on active duty."

"That looks painful."

"It is."

We looked at each other for a few minutes, the silence stretching between us. "You should go to bed, Princess," I said. My voice was thick and husky with desire. If she stayed out here much longer in those cute fucking pajamas, I'd want to take them off to discover what she was hiding underneath. Hell, who was I kidding? I already wanted to rip them off her body. She needed to get in bed before I lost all semblance of control.

She licked her lips nervously as if she knew the thoughts running through my mind. "I should," she finally answered but didn't move toward the hallway. I ground my teeth, trying to remember who she was, and how bad of an idea it was to get involved with her.

"Fuck." I leaned my hands on the island and looked away from her. She was testing my resolve in ways she didn't fucking understand. "Go now before I do something we might both regret, Princess."

Her unique eyes were wide and clouded with interest and curiosity, but she nodded and finally moved toward the back hallway. I watched her go in her damn onesie that had a giraffe's tail hanging down from her backside. Cute as fuck.

"Zeke," I called after him when I noticed he was about to go after the swinging tale like one of his chew toys. The dog stopped and gave me a disgruntled look that told me I ruined his fun. He had no idea, but I understood exactly how he felt.

Natalia gave me one last look over her shoulder before she rounded the corner and headed toward the bedrooms. It was hard to watch her go, but it was for the best. Neither one of us were in a position to start something. She had a stalker after her, and I had a motorcycle club hunting me. If there were ever two people that didn't need to get distracted and let down their guard, it was us.

Chapter Seven

Natalia

A familiar ache was pounding between my legs. Just because I'd never had a man there didn't mean that I didn't understand what was happening.

The hot, surly Mountie my parents had asked to protect me was making my lady bits tingle with untapped need. I wasn't used to that. In fact, I was almost convinced that no man would turn me on as much as the one that I made up in my head. I'd always called him Nicholas, but now he had another name and another face. Gavin.

He was strong and hot, but he was also brave and honorable. I liked that he said what needed to be said without mincing words. It took every ounce of clear thought I'd possessed to walk away from him, but now instead of a crazy stalker keeping me up. I had a hunky Mountie on my mind.

I tossed and turned a little before I decided that sleep wasn't going to come if I didn't get some relief from the building ache. It was dark in the room, and no light showed from under the door, so Gavin must have gone back to his bedroom.

I unzipped my onesie, the cold air cool against my warm skin. Relief then sleep. It was natural, and there was no way Gavin would ever know that I took matters into my own hands with him across the hall.

My nipples were hard stiff peaks. I pinched the tips and gooseflesh spread across my skin while liquid heat pooled between my legs. I slipped my right hand inside my pajamas and slowly moved my fingers between my legs.

Slick arousal coated my fingers and desire tingled through me as I glided my fingers into my wet slit. When I touched my clit, my body twitched with pleasure. It felt so good. I hadn't allowed myself to relax or felt safe enough to really indulge in my fantasies in months, but knowing I was safe and that Gavin was nearby not only had my desire churning hot, but allowed me to slip into that space in my head nobody knew about. Those fantasies that I kept hidden from everyone.

I bit my lip as I started circling my clit with my fingers, my speed picking up as I moved closer and closer to an orgasm. When I finally came, it was harder than I expected. I was always vocal when I masturbated because most of the time, I was fantasizing out loud, but I was always alone and not worried about being heard.

I cried out, surprised by how hard the orgasm was. The orgasms I'd been able to give myself have never been that hard or caused that much pleasure to short circuit my system. I shuddered and clamped my thighs around my hand. My clit was sensitive, and I needed more.

The soft knock on my door took me by surprise. Shit. I was too loud.

I bit my lip afraid to answer, hoping he would go away. He didn't.

"I know you're awake, Princess, and I know what you're doing in there. If you want me to help make the ache go away, you just have to open the door."

Did I want to open that door? Yes. I did, but I was scared to let him in—to let him know what I wanted and needed. I bit my lip again, almost to the point of pain, and slid out of bed. My pajamas were unzipped to the waist, and I slid the zipper up before I got to the door.

I turned the knob slowly, opening it. Gavin was leaning against the wall, and Zeke was sitting at his feet. He was still bare chested, and his boxers were tented. I swallowed hard seeing the proof of his arousal. His hard length was long and broad. Something you only see in a porn video.

"I didn't mean to wake you," I said softly, not taking my gaze away from his waist.

"I was up wanting you, anyway. Are you going to let me in?"

I dragged my eyes up his body and met his gaze. I nodded, slowly opening the door wider so he could come in.

"Zeke, home," Gavin said without looking away from me. I glanced down at the husky and watched as he took off back to Gavin's room.

Gavin took my hand and lifted my still damp fingers to his lips. He pulled one into his mouth, and I sucked in a sharp breath at the feel of his tongue stroking the wet flesh of my fingers.

"There's something I need to tell you first," I whispered. My desires were not the norm, that's another reason I was still a virgin because I was scared to tell anyone what I wanted and needed. If I told the wrong person, my private life could be splashed across every tabloid, and I could become the punchline to a joke on late night talk shows.

"What's that?" he asked taking my hand and leading me back farther into the room toward the bed.

"Well, two things actually." I didn't look at him because if I did, I'd lose my nerve. "First, I've never—" I swallowed hard, "With a man. I've never—"

"You're a virgin?" he said the word that seemed so hard for me to say. I was. As worldly as my profession is, and as many times as I've modeled in underwear and with men, I knew the mechanics of sex, but I've never done it.

"Yes, but there's more, though I'm not sure I should tell you." I looked nervously at anything but him.

"If you're not sure that you should, then you definitely need to tell me, Princess."

Why did I have to bring it up? Why did I have the urge to be spanked and coddled? What grown woman wanted to be little again? I was scared he would think I was a freak.

"It's nothing." I shook my head, chickening out.

"It's not nothing, Natalia. You wouldn't be so worried to tell me if it was nothing."

He saw my pajamas and didn't laugh at me. Genny was on my bed, which was a dead giveaway. My stuffed giraffe would tell him all he needed to know if he saw it, so I turned away from him and reached for my stuffie, telling him without saying the words.

"Ah," he said, understanding what I was not able to communicate to him. "You're embarrassed about your Little side?"

I gasped and met his gaze. He knew. Gavin didn't look at all shocked or surprised. Even more, he didn't look disgusted by it. "You know?"

"I figured it out, Princess. It wasn't hard."

I smiled up at him, relief flooding through my veins. "I'm getting tired, Princess, but you need some relief first. You ready to do this with Daddy?"

I nodded. "Yes."

Gavin leaned down and captured my lips in a soft drugging kiss. His lips were firm against mine, as his tongue started seeking. I felt his hands between us as he reached for the zipper on my onesie and pulled it down slowly, the fabric loosening as it traveled down its path.

He spread the fabric open and slipped it off my shoulders and down my arms until they were free. When they were, I reached up and put my arms loosely around his neck. He groaned at the contact of my breasts against his chest, and I sighed as the pajamas fell to the floor leaving me bare in front of him.

"You were naked under there." He said it more like a statement than a question, when he pulled back to see that I wasn't wearing a stitch of clothing.

"Yes. Panties are tight when you sleep." I shrugged.

"You will get no complaints from me, Princess." He held onto me as I stepped out of the footies, then led me back to the bed.

"Lay down, so Daddy can taste you properly." His voice was husky and gruff with desire, and I wanted to feel it all.

I laid back on the bed and Gavin leaned down between my thighs. He didn't waste any time teasing my already cum-soaked clit. My previous orgasm made sure I was wet, ready, and sensitive to touch.

My hips bucked against his feasting mouth as he licked and sucked at my center. It was incredible. His tongue swirled around my clit, then his lips sucked it into his mouth. His teeth nipped at the tight bud of nerves, and his fingers plunged into my pussy creating so many varying sensations that I didn't know which one to enjoy or chase.

"Oh… oh, god," I called out as my body coiled tighter. My head thrashed against the blankets and I teetered just over the edge of another release.

Gavin pushed his fingers into me and sucked hard on my clit at the same time, sending me catapulting off the edge of insanity. I cried out loud as the waves of my orgasm pulsed through me. It was unlike anything I've ever felt before, and he wasn't done yet.

He moved up my body and put his weight on his arms. Gavin winced in pain from the pressure he put on his arm. He groaned and rolled to his back.

"What's wrong?" I asked, looking at him with worry. "Is it your arm?"

"Yeah. I can't put pressure on it, Princess. It hurts too much, and I've abused it today. I have to stop." He reached up to touch my face. "As much as it pains me, Daddy can't fuck you like he wants to one handed."

I looked at his arm and trailed my eyes down his body. I didn't want him to stop either, but I didn't want him to be in pain. "Can I do it?" The question popped out before I could second guess myself.

He looked at me with hooded eyes. "Yes," he said, his voice gruff with need.

"Tell me how." I licked my lips unsure of anything but the need to have him inside me.

I watched as Daddy pulled his underwear down his hips. His long thick cock looked even bigger, standing up against his stomach.

"Come here, Princess and mount me."

Chapter Eight

Gavin

She was perfect, and I didn't ever want to fucking let her go. Natalia laid naked curled up in my arms. Her body was warm and languid next to mine.

I never expected her to want to ride me her first time out, but god, she had been magnificent when she found her pace. She was so brave and beautiful. The slow steady fucking lasted a long time, it was almost painful by the time we both went over the edge, but eventually she got us both there.

Zeke barked from the other room, so I got up and slid out of bed. Sleep had claimed us both so thoroughly after our orgasms that neither of us moved afterward. I slept better than I had in a long time, so I felt rested and got up to go find some clothes. I needed to let Zeke out and get us some breakfast.

I looked back at Natalia's sleeping body, shaking my head in awe that she actually wanted me as much as I wanted her, and she needed a Daddy as much as I needed a Little.

I grabbed my boxers from the floor and slipped them on, then quietly left the bedroom. Zeke was sitting in the hallway. He started turning in circles, his way of telling me to hurry he had to pee. "I'm coming, Buddy," I whispered and went into the bedroom to grab some warm clothes.

I needed to check out how much snow was dumped on us overnight. If it was passable, then I would expect that her family would be here soon to see her. If not, I would make her breakfast and maybe get a repeat performance of last night— maybe a few repeat performances.

I opened the back door and let Zeke out into the fenced-in backyard. He would have fun running out there and let me know when he was ready to come back in. I checked the perimeter and then used my phone to check on the streets. The storm dumped a lot of snow, but as soon as the plows went to work, her parents would be back to see her.

In the meantime, we needed to eat and get moving. I looked in the fridge and grabbed the bacon and eggs. After our exertions the night before, she would need to replenish her energy. The food was almost done when Zeke scratched at the back door. I went to let him in and saw Natalia coming down the hallway, dressed as a giraffe again. Her cheeks flushed red when our eyes met, and I couldn't keep myself from going over and giving her a kiss. She was gorgeous, and I felt something deep within me shift. Natalia Hughes owned me—my heart, body, and soul.

"Good morning, Princess," I said closing the door and ignoring the snow that Zeke had brought back in with him. "Sleep well?" I wrapped my arms around her and pulled her against my body. My dick was already stirring with interest.

"For the first time in forever, yes." She sighed and laid her head on my chest.

My phone went off, and I gave Natalia a quick kiss before moving to answer it. Elijah's face popped up on the screen, so I answered. "Yeah?"

"We've got trouble, Gavin. She was seen. Someone posted the picture on social media and tagged her stating that they love her new look."

"Fuck."

"Yeah. Someone knows she's back in Alberta, and if they know her real name, it won't be hard for them to track her down."

"Hold on," I said into the phone as I looked over at Natalia who had moved to the stove to finish the breakfast I'd started. "Nat, who all knows your real name?"

"Quite a few people know. My agent, some photographers, some models. It's not exactly a world class secret, but it's not widely known either. If someone wanted to find out, they just have to ask the right person." She turned to look at me, "Why?"

"Hopefully it's nothing," I said knowing it wasn't. That fucking picture was going to come back on us. I just knew it. Luckily, they caught the back of my head and I was unrecognizable, or we'd have a stalker and a group of bikers after us. "Did you hear?" I asked when I stepped away from her.

"Yeah. This fucker knows her last name already if he knows where she lived. The last roses and note were delivered to her apartment, not one of her sets or shows."

I angrily threaded my fingers through my hair. Yeah, he knew her last name. "I know you were trying to find out about the notes that were sent to her. Did you get copies of them yet?"

"Just the last one, and no wonder she ran. This guy is one sick fuck."

"Tell me."

"It's a perversion of a quote by Edgar Allan Poe, *'Sometimes I'm scared of my own heart; of its constant hunger for you. The way it stops and starts.'* Like I said, sick fucker. He will come after her, it's not a matter of if, but when.

"Do me a favor. Monitor all the people traveling from LAX to Edmonton or Fort McMurray. Cross reference those people with the entertainment and fashion industry. If he comes here, he'll come that way."

"You think he's going to come that quick?"

"I'm going to make damn sure he does."

"What are you thinking, Gavin?"

"I'm going to blow my own cover and kill two birds with one fucking stone."

I angrily ran my hand through my hair. This fucker terrified my girl, and I wanted him to pay. As for the mole that leaked my identity, I had my suspicions about who it was, and if I played this right, I would force the asshole out of hiding. The MC was a minor problem compared to the mole inside the Mounties. They thought I was dead, that's why I was in hiding. The only person that knew I was still alive was Elijah, the mole thought he got away with it. He would know that the MC was being watched, so they couldn't take care of the loose end. The only way he was going to get rid of me was to come and do it himself.

"You want me to watch who's traveling from more than just LAX don't you?"

"Yes. He will have to fly. A car would take too long, and I bet he'd be noticed if he was away for any length of time, so he'll have to fly. Watch for any familiar faces."

"What are you planning to do to draw them both out?"

I looked over my shoulder and saw Natalia standing there looking at me with wide eyes. She'd been listening to my conversation, but it didn't matter. She needed to know what was going on, what I was planning.

"I'm marrying a supermodel."

Chapter Nine

Natalia

My parents were shocked when they came over that afternoon to find that Gavin, and I were together. We explained that it was love at first sight, and we were going to get married as soon as we could get everything arranged. My dad wasn't happy, but my mom was thrilled. She was also not at all surprised how fast it happened for me since it was that way for her and my dad. I grew up hearing the story about how they met, and I saw how happy their marriage was over the years. I always wanted that, and I guess I got it. I just wish I knew how Gavin felt. Was it just a ruse for him, or did this feel as real to him as it felt to me?

He tapped into my sexual fantasies easily enough. After our first time together, when we weren't visiting with my family and making wedding preparations to keep up the charade or making public appearances for the sake of social media and the tabloids, we were at the safe house together. We couldn't keep our hands off each other, and every time was more explosive than the last. If Gavin's arm was in pain, I'd take his mind off of it by riding him until his cock pulsed with his orgasm inside me.

The safe house was our own cocoon of bliss, and it was just a matter of time until that cocoon was shattered. It was a sobering thought. What would happen after my stalker and the traitor that revealed Gavin's identity was caught? I wasn't sure I could go back to my life without Gavin in it.

"You okay?" Gavin asked, pulling me closer to his side as we laid snuggled in the recliner watching a movie.

"Just thinking." I shrugged and looked up at him.

"What about?"

"We haven't heard anything from Uncle E. What if this doesn't work to draw them out?"

"It will work."

"But what if it doesn't?" I insisted with a hint of frustration and aggravation in my voice. I was irritable and grouchy, and I didn't know why.

"Why don't you tell me what's really bothering you, Princess," he asked, tuning into the fact that I was worried about something beyond the plan he had in place.

"What are we going to do if it doesn't work? Are we going through with the wedding to save face because our engagement is out there now? Our upcoming marriage is trending, and I've done my best to stay out of the vicious tabloids over the years. I don't want to be a laughingstock to everyone by being dumped at the altar, and I don't want to be the crazy runaway bride. If this doesn't work, how do we defuse it without wrecking our lives?"

"How long have you been worrying about this?" he asked, sitting up and pulling me onto his lap.

"Since you told Uncle E on the phone that you were marrying me," I admitted softly, embarrassed that I hadn't said something sooner.

"Princess, you know me. Do you think I'd ever marry a woman I didn't want to marry?"

I shook my head in answer because he wouldn't.

"Do you think I'd ever embarrass you or allow someone else to embarrass you in any way?"

Again, no. He didn't like that my friends who had seen my giraffe pajamas, poked fun at me. "Do you understand what I'm telling you?" he asked, pushing me to answer.

"No." I shook my head; afraid it wasn't what I thought it was.

"Let me make it clear, then. Nobody will talk because we are getting married. I love you, Natalia."

"I love you, too."

Gavin captured my lips in a hungry kiss. The movie we were watching was forgotten as the kiss deepened and we started to tear at our clothes. My body ached with my need for him—I was insatiable where he was concerned. I'd gone from a virgin to his Little Princess in a matter of a week. God, after he spanked me for the first time, I came so hard I screamed and scared Zeke in the other room.

My body responded to him on a whole other level. Gavin knew what I needed, even when I had no clue how to ask him for it.

I stood, pushing myself away from him, and shimmied out of my leggings and panties. Gavin lifted his hips and removed his gray sweatpants, his cock bounced hotly against his six-pack abs, and I knew what I wanted.

"Fuck," he said when I lowered to my knees in front of him, half laying on the recliner's footrest.

I took his thick, velvety, soft steel cock in my hand and stroked it from root to tip. Gavin leaned his head back against the headrest, but his eyes stayed on me as he watched my hand move over his heated flesh. When I licked at the soft head of his cock, he groaned and threaded his fingers through my hair.

"Yes, Princess," he said, his voice thick with lust when I started licking around the head, taking the tip into my mouth as my hands continued to stroke his length.

My body hummed with need and excitement as I continued to pleasure him with my mouth. Gavin helped guide my movements and the pace, but I knew if I wanted to break away I could—I just didn't want to.

I looked up at him with his dick buried in my mouth. My body was on fire and needy for him. I felt my arousal on my thighs, and I shifted, trying to ease the ache between my legs, but it did no good. I needed him.

"Daddy," I said, pulling off his cock while licking and lapping at the tip like a lollipop. "I need you inside me, but I want to keep sucking you." I took his tip in my mouth and swirled my tongue over the head, lapping up the pre-cum that glistened on the top. It was a dilemma, his flavor was addicting. The power I felt giving him pleasure was exhilarating, but my pussy was empty and achy with need.

"Come here, Princess," he said, helping me to my feet. Gavin wrapped his arms around me and pulled me onto his lap. The chair forced my legs wide and rendered me unable to move. Gavin pulled my hips forward, his cock slipping inside me. My head fell back as the ecstasy of his intrusion washed over me.

Gavin used his legs to push the footrest down. The jarring of the movement made me groan as his cock dragged along the walls of my channel. It was when he pushed against the floor with his feet that I realized his intentions. Gavin used the rocking of the chair to do the work for us both.

"Oh," I said as his cock slid inside my walls with the movement of the chair. It was slow and lazy, but completely incredible. Gavin's hands went to my breast as his lips captured mine in a gentle, seductive kiss. Everything was languid and smooth.

He trailed his lips down the column of my neck and across my chest. Gavin plumped my breast with his hand and captured the stiff peak of my nipple in his mouth, sucking at the sensitized flesh. It may have been a lazy, slow fuck, but it wasn't long before I was sweating, panting, and clinging to him as my body shook and went over the edge.

We didn't move after we came. Gavin's cock stayed inside my quivering core. I leaned against him, my head on his shoulder as I tried to catch my breath. My legs were going numb from their position over the wide set recliner, but I didn't care. Gavin was still slowly rocking us while his cock still moved within me. It was a tease, and so amazingly intense at the same time.

I loved it, and I loved him.

***

I was just falling asleep when Zeke started growling a low menacing sound I'd never heard before.

"Shit," Gavin said, moving me off his lap quickly. He grunted as he picked up my weight because my legs were useless noodles from the position I'd been in for so long and he knew it. "Fuck. Fuck. Fuck."

"Gavin," I whispered, worried and not understanding what was going on.

"Can you walk?" my legs were tingling because the blood was starting to rush back through them after being in that position for so long.

It would be shaky if I got up, but something told me I needed to try—he needed me to try. I nodded and reached down for his shirt, pulling it on over my body. His shirt hung down to my upper thigh, not long enough, but longer than what my shirt would have done, and I didn't want to struggle back into my leggings.

"Get in the bathroom, lock the door, and lay in the tub. No exposure, Princess. You make yourself as small as possible and lay in the tub. Don't peek your head out and don't open the door for anyone but me."

He pulled on his sweatpants quickly, Zeke was pacing back and forth between us and the front door of the house. His growl was continuous, so something set him off and whatever it was, it wasn't good. "Go, now."

I moved toward the bathroom and looked back long enough to see him grab his gun from the drawer. He checked it, then slammed it back into the grip of the gun. His eyes met mine across the room. No words were spoken, but we said all we needed to say.

Chapter Ten

Gavin

I shouldn't have been so careless. If anything happened to Natalia, I'd never forgive myself. Zeke was a trained warning system, and one I trusted with my life. If he thought something was wrong, then something was wrong.

Quickly, I grabbed my phone and dialed Elijah. He answered after the first ring. "Yeah?"

"He's here."

"Shit," he said, his voice on alert. "Which one do you think it is?"

"Natalia's stalker wouldn't have the resources to find the safe house," I whispered, moving to the front of the house, keeping my back to the wall and out of sight of windows. "Whoever they are, they're here for me."

"I'm on my way."

"You'll never make it," I said, carefully peeking out the front blinds. To any untrained eye, nothing was amiss, but I saw what I needed to see—the snow was disturbed, as if someone was trying to cover their foot tracks as they walked around the house.

I walked down the hall and brought up the security cameras on the TV in the living room. If I could find their point of entry, I could head them off. I cycled through the black and white screens and stopped.

"I'm five minutes away, Gavin."

"It's too late," I muttered, watching the figure on the screen. "He's already inside."

I turned around, my gun held securely in my hands, the familiar weight of the weapon made it like an extension of my hand.

"I know you're there, Roth," I called out. Zeke was crouched low beside me, his teeth bared, ready to spring forward if I gave him the word. I should have sent him into the bathroom with Natalia.

Instead, she was in there with Ian Roth. The man who betrayed his country.

The door to the bathroom opened, Natalia came out, arms to her side with fear in her eyes. My heart pounded in my ears, and I wanted to take the prick apart piece by fucking piece.

"You were supposed to be dead already, Gavin."

"Sorry to disappoint you." *Come on, you fucking bastard*, I cursed silently, knowing that this situation could get Natalia killed.

"Me too." He wrapped his arm around Natalia's waist and put the gun up under her chin. His head peeked out over her shoulder and I wanted to take the shot. My finger itched to do it, but I couldn't, not until she was clear and safe.

"Why'd you do it, Roth?"

"You know why."

"Money?"

"The money was a bonus, Kincaid. I did it because had your career handed to you on a silver fucking platter. Edwards took you under his wing, and you could do no fucking wrong. I wanted to take you down a few pegs."

"Let the girl go, she has nothing to do with this."

"No, Brother," I disagree. He lifted her shirt, exposing her body to both of us. His hand touched her thigh, and she whimpered in fear. "Only you could fucking play dead and end up with Natalia fucking Van Buren."

"It wasn't planned," I said, trying to keep my eyes off the fact that his hand was hovering so close to the woman I love's pussy. He was already a dead man. I was going to kill him for putting a gun to her chin, but because his hand was on her body—I was going to beat him to death.

"Let's settle this, Roth. Once and for all. No guns. No weapons. Just like we did in the academy."

I knew he held a grudge against me when we were coming up together, but I didn't know his hatred for me ran this fucking deep. Maybe I should have kept more of an eye on him over the years, but I truly forgot about the prick after we were assigned to different field offices. I guess he kept tabs on me and my career.

I loosened my grip on the gun and lowered the weapon, hoping my show of deference would get him to let her loose. It worked, his grip loosened on her, his hand moving away from her thighs. "Your bitch's thighs are still wet. After I kill you, maybe I'll take a turn with her."

Natalia's face crumpled, contorted with fear and disgust. Zeke was waiting for the word to move, his eyes were trained on Ian.

"Call off your dog and put the gun down, then we'll go from there."

"Descendit," I gave Zeke the Latin command to stand down. He relaxed, though he was still on high alert.

"Now the gun, Gavin. Put it on the floor and kick it under the sidebar." I needed Roth to feel like he'd won—that he had me—so that he would let go of Natalia, so Zeke and I could make our move or Elijah could get here, whichever came first.

"Ok, Roth." I slowly lowered to the floor and set the gun down. My palms were out, showing him I was defenseless as I rose, "Just let her go. I'm the one you want."

Kick the gun first. He was getting more comfortable. The gun was no longer pointing at Natalia, but at me. I couldn't look at her face, so I focused on the spot just above their heads.

I gave the gun a kick, and it slid across the hard wood floor and under the sidebar. I wouldn't be able to get to it without moving the damn heavy piece of furniture, but it didn't matter. Roth still had a gun, but I had Zeke and Elijah should be on his way. He had me dead to rights, right then, because Natalia's safety was at stake. As soon as she was in the clear, he was dead.

"Alright, Natalia." He threaded his fingers through her hair and pulled hard. She cried out at the shock and pain. My gaze clashed with hers, and I almost laughed at what I saw.

Good girl. She was waiting for me to notice before she did anything. God, when this was over, I was going to kiss the hell out of that woman. Her eyes were full of fear, but there was also anger and fire written there.

"We are going to walk toward the back door." He started moving and dragging her with him even as he said it. "We're going to put the dog out. Once Zeke is safely outside and presents no threat, I'll let you go until it's time to kill you."

I looked back at Natalia, she'd have one chance to stab him with the nail file and she'd have to do it hard to do even a minimal amount of damage, but I just needed her to create a distraction before Zeke was sent outside.

She was reaching for the doorknob, Roth still had a grip on her hair, though he was allowing her more slack, so she could move.

"Now," I said, hoping she could understand my message. As soon as she I said it, Natalia's arm went back with all her might and she stabbed him in the leg. "Impetus," I said to Zeke, and he sprang into action as we both moved across the room.

Natalia pulled away from Ian. "You bitch," he said as he aimed the gun at her and fired.

Chapter Eleven

Natalia

There was blood everywhere, so much blood. Tears fell from my eyes as I pressed my hands through Zeke's fur and onto his wound. At the last second, Zeke leapt up, and the bullet hit his hindquarter.

Gavin was on top of the man he called Roth, the gun was on the floor beside him, but Gavin was pummeling him, his face was bloody, and I heard the crack of bone beneath my Daddy's fists. I couldn't bring myself to care that the man was getting beaten to death—not while Zeke was fighting for his life.

The front door burst open. Roth was unconscious on the floor beneath Gavin, so Gavin grabbed his gun and pointed it toward the front door.

"Gavin?" We both relaxed, recognizing Uncle E's voice.

"Help us," I called out, Gavin's gaze swung toward me, covered in blood. His face paled. "Zeke took the bullet. Help," I cried.

If this dog survived, he was going to live the rest of his days in the lap of luxury. I'd make sure of it.

"Natalia?" I looked up. Gavin's eyes were focused on me. "Are you hurt?"

I shook my head. "Zeke. It's all Zeke's blood."

Gavin nodded. "We'll get him to the animal hospital. Go get dressed, quickly." I ran to the bedroom and did as he said, I heard Elijah and Gavin talking, though I couldn't make out what they were saying.

My hands were covered in blood from Zeke's wound, so I tried washing them as best as I could, but I had to hurry, or he wouldn't make it. Zeke had to make it. He was a hero.

I threw the easiest clothes I had on, not caring about what it was or what it looked like. When I went back out into the living room, I was dressed in jeans and a sweater. I had no time for undergarments. Elijah had Roth cuffed, and Gavin had his coat on with his sweatpants and boots. He was using the comforter from the other bedroom to lift Zeke's still form.

"Let's go, Princess," he said while lifting Zeke up. I never thought I'd be so happy to hear the dog whimper in pain.

We sat for hours in the waiting room of the emergency animal hospital. The nurse tried to convince us to put the animal down, but we wanted him to fight for his life the way he fought for ours. Gavin and I didn't care how much it cost. That dog was going to make it. He had to.

Epilogue

Natalia

"Perfect!" I turned in the mirror to look at the back of the beautiful dress. The white lace dipped low in the back, and the smooth expanse of my back would be on display, exposed to Gavin's touch when we danced.

I loved the feel of his hands on my skin. I started thinking about him holding me as we dance at our reception, his hand caressing my back as we swayed across the floor—innocent yet arousing. The dress hugged my curves and teased just enough to tempt my groom.

"You're exquisite, My Beauty." I turned sharply at the sound of the voice—Derik. His eyes hungrily raked over my body.

"What are you doing here?" Seeing him in front of me, I knew immediately that he must be my stalker. Who else could it be? Derik must've waited for me to come out of hiding—waited until he could find out exactly where I would be before he pounced.

"I tried to tell you how perfect we were together, Natalia. We could have had it all." His voice took on an edge that sent shivers down my spine.

What do I do? I asked myself. "I'm sorry, Derik. I fell in love with someone else."

He ran his fingers through his perfect hair, frustrated with my answer. Derik was getting agitated, and I knew that didn't bode well for the situation.

"Hey." I forced a smile. "Why don't you go sit out in the church and stay for the wedding? We'd love to have you here." *Right where Gavin and Elijah can arrest you,* I added silently.

"This is supposed to be our wedding, Natalia. We were supposed to take the fashion industry by storm, just the two of us. The it couple. You ruined my plans." His voice had risen on the last part of his tirade. I prayed someone heard, and I lucked out because the next thing I knew the locked door splintered as it was kicked in.

Gavin had Derik pressed against the wall, his arm a solid band across the other man's shoulders. Derik was sobbing and screaming about how I betrayed him, and I ruined everything.

I covered my mouth with my hand, fear clutching my stomach in a vice. He was demented, and I was on the verge of puking. How could he think that we were anything to each other? We shot photos together once, and I was retiring from the industry to have a family and a normal life outside of the public eye. I'd accomplished what I wanted to in my professional world, now I wanted to accomplish my goals in my personal life. I wanted a home with Gavin and kids.

Part of me felt sorry for him, he was clearly sick and needed help. Gavin handed him over to Uncle E and some Mounties I hadn't met yet. They were all in their formal, red uniforms that matched Gavin's. I loved his formal uniform.

When it was just us in the room, he hugged me. "Are you okay, Princess?"

"Relieved, it's over—truly over."

"It is. The guys are going to take him into custody, so we can still get married. Are you ready?"

I nodded and put Derik out of my mind. Despite him, this was going to be the happiest day of my life. "Yes."

Gavin gave me a long lingering kiss before he pulled back and kissed my forehead. "I'll see you at the end of the aisle, Princess. Don't leave me waiting too long."

"I'm right behind you, Daddy."

***

The crowd stood as I approached the back doors of the church. My father held my arm tightly, but it felt like me and Gavin were the only ones in the room, because all I could see in front of me was my Mountie at the end of the aisle with his four-legged best man, and the twenty steps I still needed to take to reach him, and start our off this new adventure together. Just a Little Princess, her Daddy, and of course Zeke.

The End

Other Works by Annelise Reynolds

Dark Leopards MC South Texas Book 2

Blind Spot

mybook.to/blindspot

Volkov Bratva trilogy

Nikolai

https://amzn.to/3aLfKTv

Steel Demons MC Book 1

Phoenix Bar

mybook.to/PhoenixBar

Steel Demons MC Book 2

Ember's Burn

mybook.to/EmbersBurn

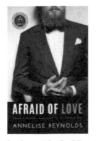

Bid on Love Bachelor #8 & Hard to Love Series
Book 1

Afraid of Love
mybook.to/AfraidofLove

Ridin' Nerdy
mybook.to/ridinnerdy

Holiday Heartthrob Book 1

Bidding on Santa

mybook.to/BiddingOnSanta

Holiday Heartthrob Book 2

Stupid Cupid

mybook.to/StupidCupid

Holiday Heartthrob Book 3

Christmas Calamity

mybook.to/ChristmasCalamity

Holiday Heartthrob Book 4

Love & Fireworks

http://mybook.to/loveandfireworks

Forever Safe Summer II

Heatwave

mybook.to/Heatwave

Fall in Love Forever Safe Series

Kink 101

http://mybook.to/kink101

Sweet Treats

mybook.to/SweetTreats

Collaborative Works with Dawn Sullivan

Christmas of Love Collaboration

Wedding Bell Rock

mybook.to/WeddingBellRock

Author Bio

I spend my days working, my evenings with my two wonderful kids, and my nights are when the characters in my head are given free reign. The tagline for Phoenix Bar, "Beauty After the Burn", holds special meaning for me and really helped to give birth to the story. Like Phoenix, I've had to rebuild my life from the ashes. It's been a long journey with a roller coaster of emotions and stresses, but I can truly say where my life is now is more beautiful than where it was. I am fulfilling my lifelong dream of being an author.

Author Links

Follow me on Amazon
Like my Facebook Page
Join her group Annelise's Fiery Vixens
Visit her Website
Follow on her Bookbub
Follow her on Goodreads

Made in United States
Troutdale, OR
10/22/2023